MICHAEL ROSEN is an enormously successful writer, poet, scriptwriter, performer and broadcaster. Winner of the Smarties Award, the Other Award and the Signal Poets Award, he has written more than a hundred children's books, including *Uncle Billy Being Silly* and *Centrally Heated Knickers* (both Penguin), *When Did You Last Wash Your Feet?* (Collins), *Even More Nonsense* (Hodder) and, for Frances Lincoln, *Songbird Story*. In 1997 he won the Eleanor Farjeon Award for his outstanding contribution to children's literature.

PRISCILLA LAMONT studied graphic design at Canterbury College of Art. A full-time artist, she is a portrait painter as well as a successful children's book illustrator. Her recent titles include *Our House* and *Where's My Mum?* (both Walker), *Will There be Polar Bears?* (Reed), *Playtime Rhymes* (Dorling Kindersley) and a series of nine books for the Cambridge Reading Scheme.

*It seems incredible but this book was written before my son
Eddie died and before the new baby was born two years later.
So I dedicate it to Elsie and lovely old Eddie. – M.R.*

To Leo and Molly – P.L.

First published in Great Britain in 2002 by
Frances Lincoln Limited, 4 Torriano Mews,
Torriano Avenue, London NW5 2RZ

British Library Cataloguing in Publication Data available on request

ISBN 0-7112-1488-3 hardback
ISBN 0-7112-1489-1 paperback

Printed in Singapore

3 5 7 9 8 6 4 2

Lovely Old Roly

Michael Rosen
Illustrated by Priscilla Lamont

FRANCES LINCOLN

Poor Roly!
His legs are tired. His whiskers are sad.
He sleeps all day.
"I think he's going," said Dad.
We'll sit with you, Roly.

Poor Roly!
His fur is dry. His eyes are old.
"I think it's nearly time," said Mum.
We love you, Roly.

Poor Roly!
He died on the Tuesday.
We buried him in the evening.
Goodbye, lovely old Roly!

"Has he really gone now?" we said.
"Yes, but you won't ever forget him,"
said Dad.
"He'll always be in and around you
somewhere," said Mum.
Old Roly.

So we tried to play
What's the Time, Mr Wolf?
We tried to play Pogo Sticks.
And we even tried to play
Danger Dog.
But Roly was too near.

Mum said things
had to be done.
Breakfasts and bedtimes
and shopping.
That sort of stuff.

Breakfasts
and bedtimes
and shopping.

"Can we have a kitten?" we said.
"Can we have a puppy?" we said.
"Can we have a rabbit?" we said.

And it was no, not yet,
it's too soon.
Poor us!

So we played
What's the Time, Mr Wolf?,
and Pogo Sticks,
and Danger Dog.

Then, one day...
"Mum, there's a cat at the door!"
"I think she's hungry."
"Can we feed her?"
"She wants to come in."

And it was maybe,
all right, a little –
but outside. Not inside.

"Mum, the cat's here again!"
"I think she's hungry."
"Can we feed her?"
"She wants to come in."
And it was maybe,
all right, a little –
but outside. Not inside.

But – too late!
She was in, sniffing and
sneaking all over the place.

"Come here, cat!"

"Over here, cat!"

"On me, cat!"

And cat came to stay.
We called her Sausage,
because she's a sausage on legs.
A roly-poly sausage.
And Sausage plays
What's the Time, Mr Wolf?,
and Pogo Sticks,
and Danger Dog.

"I wonder why Sausage
came here?" said Dad.
"She knew this was a house
with no cat," said Mum.
"She knew this was a house
that wanted a cat," we said.

And Sausage is with us a lot.

Loads and loads and loads.

Very nearly all the time.

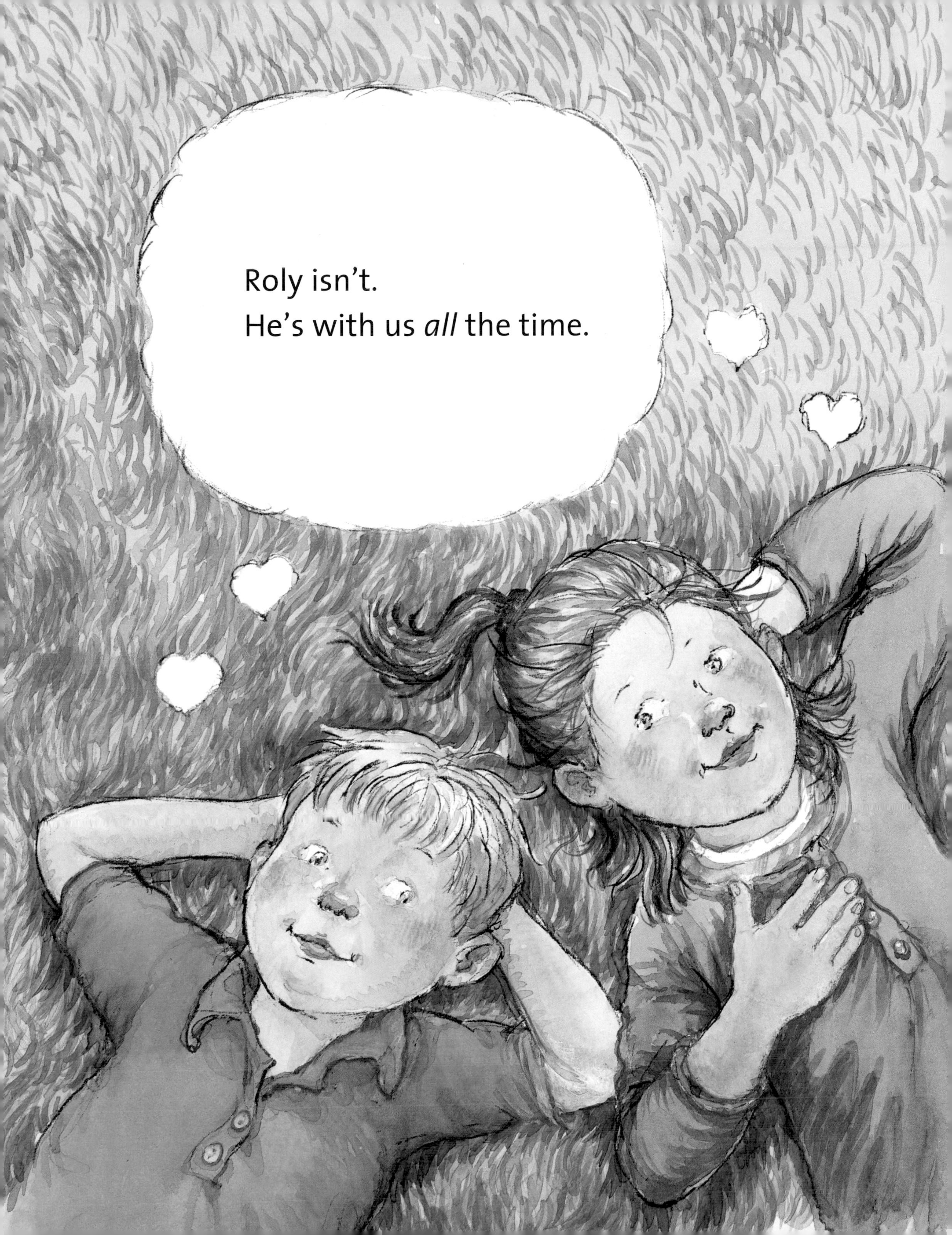
Roly isn't.
He's with us *all* the time.

MORE TITLES AVAILABLE IN PAPERBACK FROM FRANCES LINCOLN

Chimp and Zee

Catherine and Laurence Anholt

"Ha ha ha! Hee hee hee!" Come and meet Chimp and Zee, the cheekiest, most energetic twins in Jungletown!

Suitable for Nursery Education and Early Years Education
Suitable for National Curriculum English – Reading, Key Stage 1
Scottish Guidelines English Language – Reading, Level A

ISBN 0-7112-1897-8 £6.99

How to be a Cat

Mary Hoffman
Illustrated by Pam Martins

A mother cat teaches her kittens everything they need to know, including yawning, stretching and careful washing, in this charming story by Mary Hoffman.

Suitable for National Curriculum English – Reading, Key Stages 1 and 2
Scottish Guidelines English language – Reading, Level A

ISBN 0-7112-1901-X £5.99

I Have Feelings

Jana Novotny Hunter
Illustrated by Sue Porter

"Waking up is my best time – then I'm feeling HAPPY. And when we go to the park I feel really EXCITED!" Small children will fall in love with the adorable star of *I Have Feelings!* – an essential book for learning to express your emotions.

Suitable for Nursery Education and Early Years Education
Scottish Guidelines English Language – Reading, Level A

ISBN 0-7112-1734-3 £5.99

Frances Lincoln titles are available from all good bookshops
Prices are correct at time of publication, but may be subject to change